The Quiltmaker's Journey

CROSSBILLS

SNOW BUNTING

Attic Window

WOOD PIGEON

KINGFISHER

EAGLE OWL

LITTLE OWL

Vegetable Soup

Air Castle

MAGPIE

CRESTED TIT

Providence

GREY HERON

BLUE THROAT

REDSTART

Twist and Turn

CUCKOO

NIGHTINGALE

Moon Over the Mountain

WOODCHAT SHRIKE

Bright Side

EUROPEAN ROBIN

BARN SWALLOW

WALL CREEPER

NUTHATCH

Depression

TURTLEDOVE

GREEN WOODPECKER

The Castle Wall

CRANE

HOUSE SPARROW

BLUE TIT

Old Home

QUAIL   STARLING

Apple Tree

GOLDEN ORIOLE   JAY

Home Again

SPARROW HAWK

GREAT GREY SHRIKE

GLOSSY IBIS

Bird's Nest

ROOK

BLACK WOODPECKER

Silver and Gold

WHITE-THROATED DIPPER

I Wish You Well

ROLLER

ROSE-RINGED PARAKEET

Bright Hopes

SISKIN

HOODED CROW

Autumn Leaf in Delectable Mountains

HOOPOE

ROSEFINCH

Miller's Daughter

BLACK-HEADED GULL

BLACK TERN

The Thorny Thicket

COMMON TERN

WHITE-WINGED TERN

Beacon Lights

The Quiltmakers Journey

STORY BY **Jeff Brumbeau**

PICTURES BY

Gail de Marcken

SCHOLASTIC INC.
New York Toronto London Auckland Sydney
Mexico City New Delhi Hong Kong Buenos Aires

SPECIAL THANKS TO BARBARA BRACKMAN FOR HER BOOK *ENCYCLOPEDIA OF PIECED QUILT PATTERNS*,
IN WHICH GAIL DE MARCKEN FOUND ALL OF THE QUILT PATTERNS
USED IN *THE QUILTMAKER'S JOURNEY*.

ISBN 0-439-79171-5

12 11 10 9 8 7 6 5 4 3 2   5 6 7 8 9 10/0

Printed in the U.S.A.   40

First Scholastic paperback printing, October 2005

The artwork is rendered in watercolor.

To Marcia, who travels the earth with love as her compass

—Jeff

For Marina and Carl, Natasha and Aaron, and Paya,

all of whom have recognized walls

and chosen to live beyond them

—Gail

You may have once heard the story of a quiltmaker who lived in a wee house on the side of a mountain, her only neighbors the sun and the moon and the stars. Each day she toiled away on the beautiful quilts that all said were the loveliest in the land.

Few had ever seen her, a lost shepherd, a wandering wood-cutter or two. But many knew who she was by her deeds. They said she was the most gifted and giving woman ever known, and that she could have grown immensely rich by selling her wondrous quilts. But she would only give them to those in need. And so, every night by the last of the candle-light, the quiltmaker was remembered in the prayers of many.

But if by luck you should happen upon her, and ask if she had always been such a giving person, the quiltmaker would tell you that she was once quite different indeed. As a young woman, she gave no thought to people in need. It was not that she was selfish, but because she and all the children of the town had lived their lives in a world where poverty was unknown.

A great stone wall, thick and high, had been built around the town. The children had never seen what was outside, but the town Elders warned that there was something terrible out there, something too awful to speak of. They told them to never, ever even think about looking for a way to the other side. And so, for many a night, the young would tremble in their beds, fearful of the creatures they imagined lay waiting just outside the walls.

Because all the people of her town were rich, the girl thought the same was true of everyone in the world. Her parents had died and left her a fantastic fortune, and her life was very much like that of a princess. Everything she needed, she had. Everything she wanted, she was given. So incredibly wealthy was she that one day she simply ran out of things to buy.

The house where she lived was grand and tall—so tall that it cast a shadow on all the others in the town below. Each and every meal was a feast, with delectables piled high on a table so long that waiters needed bicycles to get from one end to the other. She was never cold or ever hungry, and always safe from harm. Yet, she was as unhappy as she was rich.

Often, she would visit with the seamstress, who made her gowns and had taught her how to make pretty little things with cloth and thread. One day as they sat together in the attic sewing room, the older woman could see that the girl was sad.

"What is it that makes your mouth turn down so?" she asked her.

"Oh, I just don't know. I have everything anyone could ever want, friends who love me, and a wonderful party to go to each night of the week. Yet, even with so much, my heart feels empty. It seems as if there should be something more. I feel that I'm meant to do something important with my life. But I just don't know what it is."

"Don't worry," said the seamstress as she hugged her. "You'll find your way."

"But how?"

"Is it near or far? Is it right there before you to see? I cannot say for sure. But I do know you've already begun your journey."

Now, ever since she was quite young, the girl had always been known for her bravery. She'd be the first to dare to climb the tallest tree, dance beneath the wildest rainstorm, or stand up to anyone for what she believed. And so, for some time, she had thought about stealing outside the wall to see just what the horrors were that lurked there. She knew the Elders would be furious, but her friends would love the stories she brought back.

It had always been said by some that far below the town hall there was a secret passageway. And that, if you were bold enough to venture inside, it would lead you to the world beyond the wall. However the stories went, those who had gone in had become lost forever.

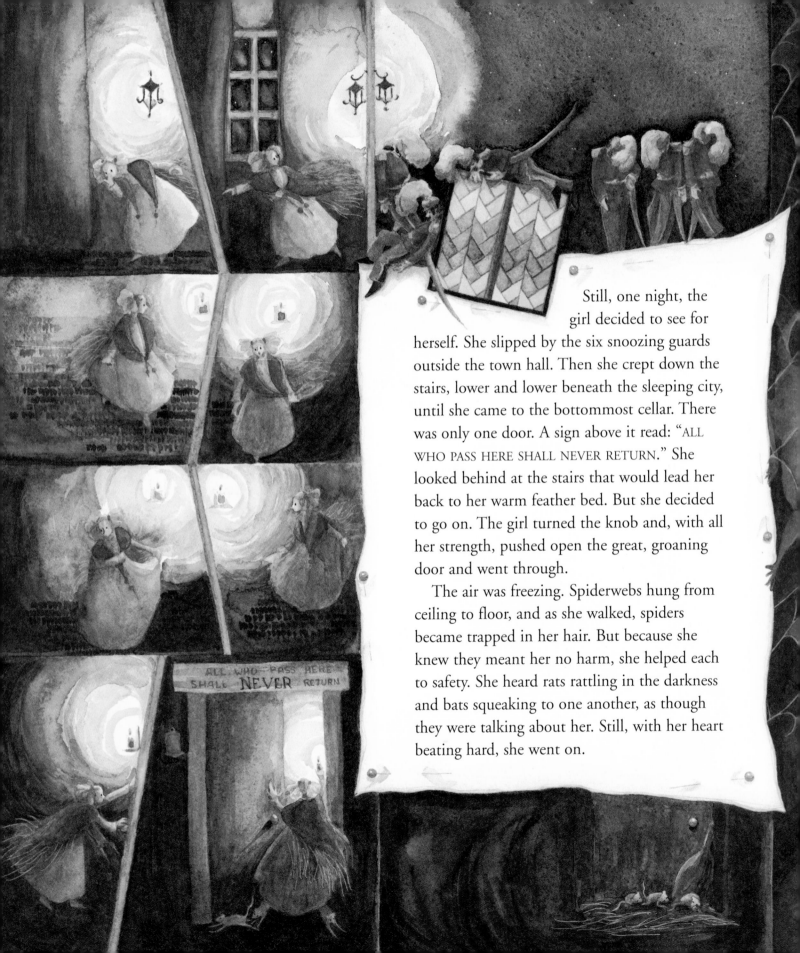

Still, one night, the girl decided to see for herself. She slipped by the six snoozing guards outside the town hall. Then she crept down the stairs, lower and lower beneath the sleeping city, until she came to the bottommost cellar. There was only one door. A sign above it read: "ALL WHO PASS HERE SHALL NEVER RETURN." She looked behind at the stairs that would lead her back to her warm feather bed. But she decided to go on. The girl turned the knob and, with all her strength, pushed open the great, groaning door and went through.

The air was freezing. Spiderwebs hung from ceiling to floor, and as she walked, spiders became trapped in her hair. But because she knew they meant her no harm, she helped each to safety. She heard rats rattling in the darkness and bats squeaking to one another, as though they were talking about her. Still, with her heart beating hard, she went on.

Then, she came to a place where the passageway led in several different directions. She chose her path and pressed on until, finally, her candle burned out. Alone in the darkness, she became confused and could not tell which way was which. She couldn't even guess how to return the way she'd come. But she was determined to go on.

Then, just ahead, she spied a candle burning. When she reached the candle, another suddenly appeared beyond it. She had no idea what this mysterious magic might be, but one by one the candles led her through the gloomy passageway to the other side of the wall. When she finally came out, it was already morning. And what she saw was terrible indeed.

There were people in ragged clothes. Some lay on the ground without bed or blanket or pillow, others cried of hunger. She saw houses too old to keep a body warm. And there were children who had run out of tears to cry.

She went on, expecting to see a dragon or something just as frightening as the Elders had led her to believe. But there was nothing of the sort. For days she walked, passing through more and more villages much like the first. There was unhappiness and helplessness everywhere. The world, she sadly realized, was not as she had thought it was.

Finally, tired, she lay down in a field to sleep. But when the girl awoke, she discovered that she'd gone so far she had no idea where her town was anymore.

"How will I ever find my way?" the girl wondered. "What will I eat?" Still, she knew she must be strong, and so, started on her way.

But the girl need not have worried. All along the way, she found that the people she'd been afraid of were kind to her. She learned that it wasn't them, but living in need that was frightful.

They were happy to help her in any way. If they had little in their pantries, they gave what they could. If they had nothing, they gave from their hearts.

Over the winding, rising road she traveled. When her fine shoes fell away in scraps, a passing girl asked her where she was going. After listening to her tale, she took off her own shoes, the only pair she owned, and gave them to the barefoot girl.

"But, I—I can't take your only pair of shoes," she replied.

"Oh, please," the ragged girl said with a smile. "I know what it's like to be far from home. I just hope they carry you there all the faster."

One day, as she trudged along, a junkman, pulling a cart piled high, stopped her and pulled out the only thing of value he carried. "I have no bread or horse to help you on your journey. But I can give you this rose. When you feel tired or hopeless, its beauty will remind you that wonderful things may arise in the next bend of the road."

When she had gone longer than ever with nothing to eat, she found an apple tree with just a few pieces of fruit left on its branches. She gathered the apples in her skirts and, hungry though she was, decided to walk on and save them til night. But she'd not gone far when she passed an old woman sleeping beside the road. Her face was thin and her fingers crooked with age. The young girl felt badly for the woman, so she decided to leave an apple for her to find when she woke. Then, down the road, there was someone else, and then another in need. To each she gave an apple until she found that there was nothing left for herself.

But, the young girl now realized, she no longer felt hungry. Instead, it was as though she'd eaten a whole basket full of fruit, so full of happiness she felt from these little gifts she'd given!

Now, she saw the world as it truly was. And so she knew where her happiness lay. But before she could go find her new life, she must first face the town Elders and their lies.

She walked for many days. Although it seemed like the town would never appear, at last she saw it before her. It rose glittering and grand into the sky. Her return was the talk of the town and a majestic celebration was announced for that very day. But before it could begin, the young lady marched straight to the town hall. The Elders stood tall and stern before her. She spoke for a long time about all the people who lived outside the town, near and far, who needed their help.

"Oh, just ignore the poor,"
one of the Elders said.

"If they wanted to be rich, well, then they
shouldn't have been born poor," added another.

"Now, my dear," said a third, "you should
know that if you don't look at those people,
then you don't have to think about them.
That's why we built the wall around us in
the first place."

"Well," she said. "I can never be happy
here with so much when there are so many
in the world with so little." The young lady
then told them that she had decided to leave
the town so she could help these people.

A clamor arose among the Elders. No one
had ever dared leave the town before. At last,
one spoke. "If you go," he said, "know this:
You shall lose all that you own and never be
allowed to return. You will be banished with
nothing."

But she knew what was in her heart, and she knew what would finally bring her happiness. Her plan had been to use her riches to help those in need. Now, all she had to give was herself. So she walked away, from her friends and the only home she had ever known. And she carried nothing but the clothes she wore and the ring (which she had hidden away) that her mother had given her long ago.

Now, her bed was an armful of leaves, her comb a handful of twigs, her dinner a mouthful of whatever the earth would grant her.

One day, she came upon a man whose small field of corn would not grow. But she did not know how to help him.

Beside the wild ocean, she watched a fisherman whose nets caught no fish. But she did not know how to help him.

She met a family whose tiny old house was falling down. But she did not know how to help them.

She wandered on,
wondering what gift,
if any, was hers to give.
Then, early one dawn as she neared another
strange town, she saw a single candle burning
in the distance. She followed its light over field
and forest and eventually discovered a mother
and son huddled in a doorway, shivering in
their sleep. The young lady would have liked
to cover them with something warm, but she
had neither blanket nor coat.

And then at last she knew what she could do.

Early the next morning,
as soon as the shops opened
their doors, she sold her beloved
ring—the last thing her mother had given her.
Then she bought needles and thread and cloth.

Looking for just the right place to work, a
great mountain drew her up upon its shoulders.
The aspens' leaves had fallen and dressed the
forest in gold. The girl followed a path made
by deer, and was brought to a meadow near
the top of the mountain. Here, the trees gently
swayed and waved a welcome in the wind.
Beneath one she found the perfect place for her
work. Someone long ago had made a chair out
of stones and left it for whomever should pass
by the mountain. It was so high up that she felt
she could have a chat with the man in the
moon. Right away she set to work.

Now, the seamstress had
taught her to make lots of
pretty things—little pillows
and handkerchiefs and such.
But the young lady had decided to make a
quilt for the mother and son. It had to be one,
most certainly, that was very warm. But it had
to be something else as well, and this was very
important. It must be beautiful—so beautiful
that the quilt would make the two feel loved,
not forgotten, if only for just a moment.

The young lady was afraid that she wouldn't
be able to make the quilt she'd seen in her dream.
But as she worked and worked and time passed,
it seemed as though something magical had
touched her. The sun had never seemed warmer,
or the sky bluer. Her hands, awkward at first for
lack of practice, soon flew like young, darting
sparrows. And all the while she felt as though
invisible angels guided her eye and her needle.
In this way the quilt slowly came to be.

Though she had wondered how she'd be able to live with nothing, she need not have. One morning, as she bent over her work, a grandfather squirrel surprised her with a gift of nuts. A wild, but mild, boar brought carrots that it had gathered especially for her. Another time, a bustling brown mother bear presented her with a honeycomb. Then, a duck arrived with her five well-behaved ducklings, all waddling along in a row, quack-quack-quacking their hellos. Each carried a big raspberry in its beak.

And if rain should threaten, a flock of birds of every known kind would gather above the tree where she worked. Together they would spread their wings like a great, chattering umbrella above her.

And, sure enough,
out of the hours and bits
of cloth and cotton thread,
a lovely quilt came to be. It
had the colors of hopeful mornings
and rosy-cheeked children and gardens bursting
in bloom. The quilt was ready.

Though it was dark, she put the quilt under
her arm and stumbled down the path to look
for the poor mother and son. And then, the man
in the moon came out, as though he'd heard tell
of her plight and sought to light her way.

The quiltmaker found
the two asleep in each other's
arms. So as not to wake them,
she carefully wrapped her gift tight
and right around them. When they
began to stir, the quiltmaker quickly hid.

Both mother and son woke with a start, and
then cried with delight at so marvelous a gift. They
looked all about to see who could have given them
such a fine thing. But there was no one. And so, in
time, they wearily closed their eyes and then slept,
now warm, now hopeful, beneath their new quilt.

They would never know it was she who had
made them this gift, though, because the
quiltmaker didn't think it important. All they'd
be sure of—like many, many others in need in the
years to come—was that someone, somewhere in
the world, cared for them.

And so, having found her way and her gift, the
quiltmaker settled on the great mountain she liked
so well. She worked steadily through the seasons
of the passing years on her wonderful quilts. When
finished with each, she left her gifts of warmth and
hope in the hands of someone in need.

Now, after hearing the quiltmaker's tale, you still might look at her tiny house and faded clothes and feel sad for her. But her quick smile and knowing eyes would tell you that you must not have heard her story well. Because she might have had little, but she had everything she'd ever need to be happy.

KESTREL

BULLFINCH

LONG-EARED OWL

BARN OWL

GOLDEN EAGLE

Right and Left

Sunburst

Beginner's Choice

GREENFINCH

GOLDFINCH

MOORHEN

TUFTED DUCKS

WHITE STORK

BEE-EATER

Wild Duck

Mariner's Compass

PHEASANT

GREAT SPOTTED WOODPECKER

Honeycomb

Girl's Joy

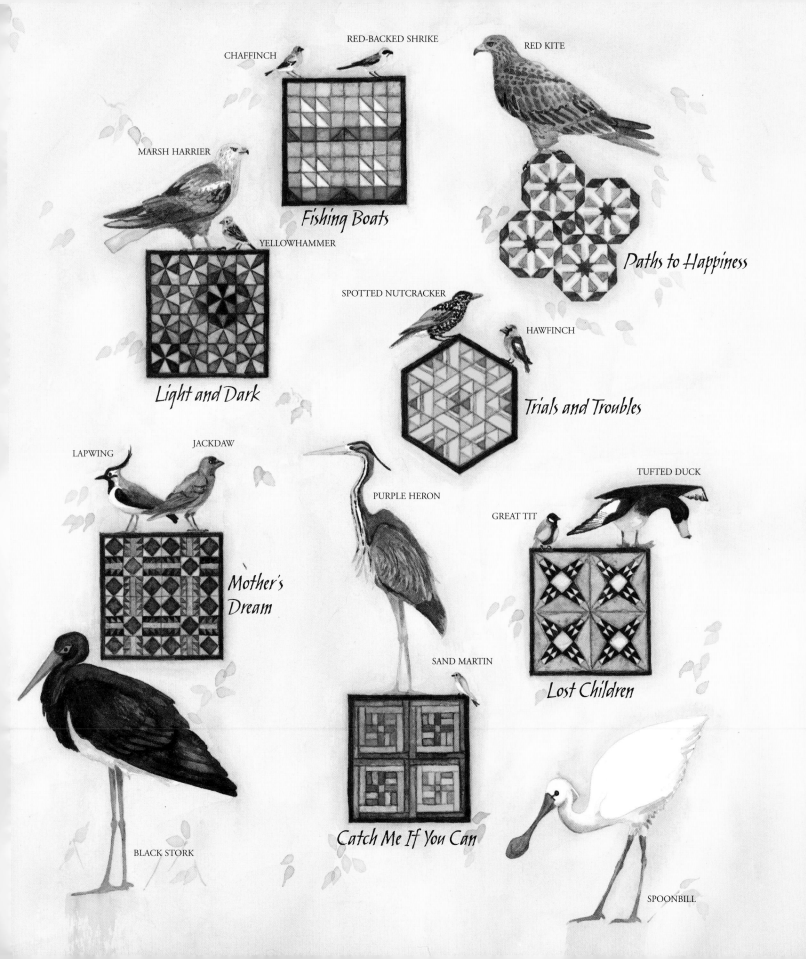

CHAFFINCH

RED-BACKED SHRIKE

RED KITE

MARSH HARRIER

YELLOWHAMMER

Fishing Boats

Paths to Happiness

Light and Dark

SPOTTED NUTCRACKER

HAWFINCH

Trials and Troubles

LAPWING

JACKDAW

TUFTED DUCK

GREAT TIT

PURPLE HERON

Mother's Dream

Lost Children

BLACK STORK

SAND MARTIN

Catch Me If You Can

SPOONBILL